The Iroko-man

A Yoruba Folktale

retold by

PHILLIS GERSHATOR

illustrated by

HOLLY C. KIM

Orchard Books
New York

Text copyright © 1994 by Phillis Gershator
Illustrations copyright © 1994 by Holly C. Kim
All rights reserved. No part of this book may be reproduced or transmitted in any form or
by any means, electronic or mechanical, including photocopying, recording or by any
information storage or retrieval system, without permission in writing from the Publisher.

Orchard Books, 95 Madison Avenue, New York, NY 10016

Manufactured in the United States of America. Printed by Barton Press, Inc.
Bound by Horowitz/Rae. Book design by Mina Greenstein
The text of this book is set in 15 point Souvenir Medium. The illustrations are compositions
of painted cut papers. 10 9 8 7 6 5 4 3 2 1

Library of Congress Cataloging-in-Publication Data
Gershator, Phillis. The Iroko-man : a Yoruba folktale / retold by Phillis Gershator ;
illustrated by Holly C. Kim.   p.   cm. "A Richard Jackson book"—Half t.p.
Summary: When the terrifying Iroko-man tries to take a woodcarver's first-born child as
partial payment for bringing fertility to his village, the father must find a clever solution.
ISBN 0-531-06810-2. ISBN 0-531-08660-7 (lib. bdg.)
[1. Folklore, Yoruba.] I. Kim, Holly C., ill. II. Title. PZ8.1.G353Ir 1994
398.21—dc20 [E] 93-4888

To my father, Morton Dimondstein,
for the sandpaper leaves, woodcarver's tools,
and exposure to the art of Africa
—P.G.

To my dearest mom and dad with all my love,
and my special thanks to God
—H.C.K.

In the beginning, the Earth Goddess planted the iroko tree, first tree in the land—before the silk-cotton tree, before the mahogany and the kola. And there, in one of the oldest and tallest iroko trees, a man-spirit made his home.

The Iroko-man hollowed out a sleeping place in the trunk, and he dug holes in the hard wood to hide his precious iroko stones. Sometimes, when he had nothing better to do, he gathered up his stones and counted them.

At night he carried a torch and prowled around the woods, scaring travelers to death. Anyone who looked at the Iroko-man face-to-face went mad and died.

His magic was powerful, both for good and for evil.

Once, in a village in Nigeria, it happened that no children had been born for many years. The people longed for children, and finally, when even songs and prayers did not break the spell, the young women asked the spirit in the iroko tree to help them.

Hoping for good magic, the young women gathered
around in a circle, with their backs to the tree.

"Please, Iroko-man, help to lift this spell upon our
village. Let children be born," they begged.

"What will you give me if I do?" he asked.

Most of the women were farmers' wives. They
promised him gifts of corn, yams, fruit, goats, and
sheep. Oluronbi was the woodcarver's wife. She had
none of these things to offer the Iroko-man. In
desperation she said, "I will bring you my firstborn
child."

Nine months later the women all gave birth. Once again a baby's cry was heard in the village, and the people rejoiced.

Oluronbi and her husband loved their beautiful child so much, they could not bear to give it to the Iroko-man. They knew that once the baby looked at him, face-to-face, the baby was sure to go mad and die.

Meanwhile, the other women took their gifts of corn, yams, fruit, goats, and sheep and laid them around the foot of the iroko tree.

The women dared not look at him, but they heard him stamp his feet and chant gaily,

"I am the Iroko-man.
I always have my way.
I am the Iroko-man
and everyone must pay."

Oluronbi stayed behind. She did not keep her promise to the Iroko-man. Instead, she held the baby close to her and wept, fearful of what might happen.

But nothing terrible happened. Months passed, and the baby grew strong and healthy. Oluronbi almost forgot about the Iroko-man.

One day, when Oluronbi was walking through the forest, the Iroko-man jumped out of the iroko tree and grabbed her. He shouted, "Where is the child? Bring it to me!"

"I cannot! I cannot!" she cried.

He stamped his feet and chanted angrily,

"I am the Iroko-man.
I <u>always</u> have my way.
I am the Iroko-man
and <u>everyone</u> must pay."

He was so angry, he transformed Oluronbi into a little bird. The little bird flew up into the tree, singing sadly,

"One promised corn.
One promised yams.
One promised fruit.
One promised goats.
One promised sheep.
And one, poor Oluronbi,
promised a child.
She did not pay
and now in this tree
she will forever stay."

When Oluronbi did not come home, her husband, the woodcarver, searched for her in the forest. He saw no trace of his wife, but, as he passed the iroko tree, he heard a little bird singing sadly,

"One promised corn.
One promised yams.
One promised fruit.
One promised goats.
One promised sheep.
And one, poor Oluronbi,
promised a child.
She did not pay
and now in this tree
she will forever stay."

The woodcarver knew then that the Iroko-man had taken his wife and turned her into a bird, all because she had not brought him her newborn child.

He thought and thought. How could he satisfy the Iroko-man without giving up their baby? Then he had an idea.

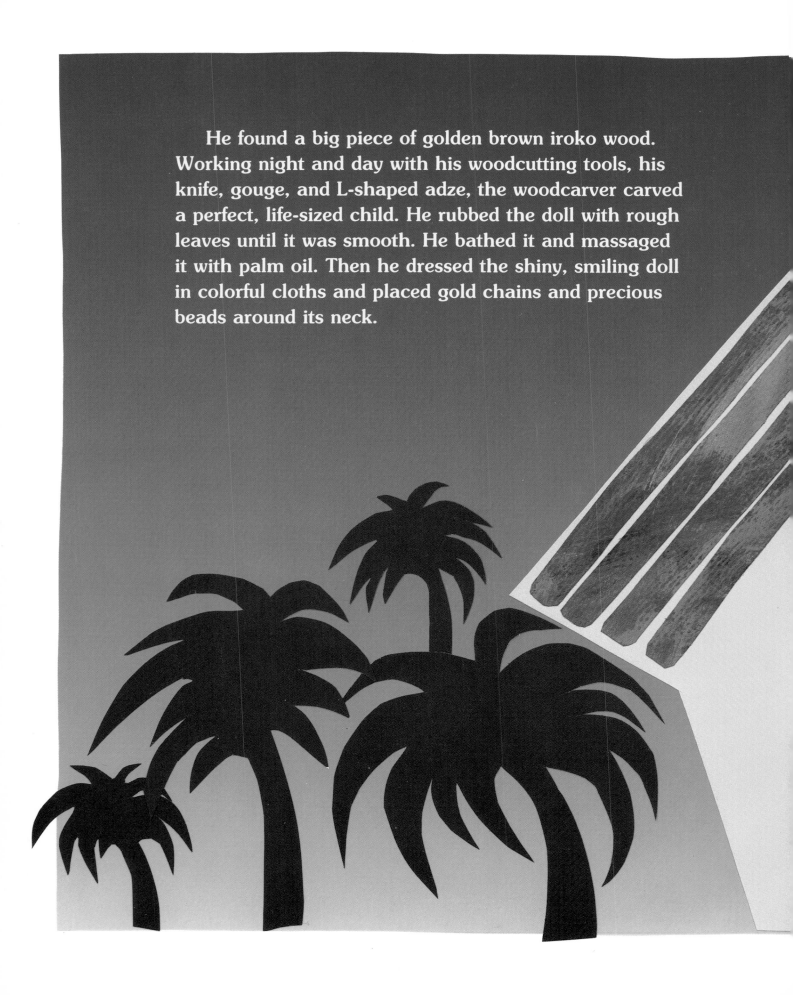

He found a big piece of golden brown iroko wood.
Working night and day with his woodcutting tools, his
knife, gouge, and L-shaped adze, the woodcarver carved
a perfect, life-sized child. He rubbed the doll with rough
leaves until it was smooth. He bathed it and massaged
it with palm oil. Then he dressed the shiny, smiling doll
in colorful cloths and placed gold chains and precious
beads around its neck.

The woodcarver laid the wood doll at the foot of the iroko tree.

As soon as he saw the baby, the Iroko-man transformed the sadly singing bird back into a woman. He picked up the shiny new, sweetly smelling doll and held it in his arms. He danced around with it, chanting joyfully,

> *"I am the Iroko-man.*
> *I always have my way.*
> *I am the Iroko-man*
> *and everyone must pay."*

He was happy with the child, for it did not go mad when he looked into its face, and it never cried for its mother and father. It always obeyed when he told it not to touch his precious stones. And best of all, it smiled all the time.

The Iroko-baby was good company for the Iroko-man, the spirit who lived in the tree.

AUTHOR'S NOTE

THIS IS an adaptation of the story "Oluronbi" in *Yoruba Legends* by M. I. Ogumefu (London: The Sheldon Press, 1929; reprinted by AMS Press in New York).

The iroko tree is *Chlorophora excelsa,* native to West Africa. It is also called the African oak and Nigeria teak. Its timber is valuable and is used for shipbuilding and furniture. Strange but true, a small number of the trees contain lumps of calcium carbonate, called iroko stones, hard enough to dull woodworking tools. Like other sacred old trees in Nigeria, certain irokos are filled with souls of the newborn.